LONG-ARM QUARTERBACK

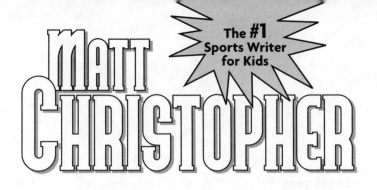

The #1
Sports Writer
for Kids

LONG-ARM
QUARTERBACK

Little, Brown and Company
Boston   New York   London

First Edition

Library of Congress Cataloging-in-Publication Data

Christopher, Matt.
    Long-arm quarterback / Matt Christopher. — 1st ed.
        p.   cm.
    Summary: Twelve-year-old Cap Wadell wants to play on a "real"
football team, but his middle school in a small Texas town does not
have enough players — until his grandfather revives interest in the
game of six-man football.
    ISBN 0-316-10571-6 (hc) — ISBN 0-316-10562-7 (pb)
    [1. Six-man Football — Fiction.   2. Football — Fiction.]
I. Title.
PZ7.C458L1   1999
[Fic.] — dc21   99-26049

10 9 8 7 6 5 4 3 2 1

MV-NY

Printed in the United States of America

To
Craig, Diane,
Paul, and Karen

LONG-ARM
QUARTERBACK

1

The football flew in a smooth arc with no wobble at all. Candy Wadell sprinted hard, looking over her shoulder for the ball.

"Look at that ball *fly!*" Grandpa Tully Wadell sat on his favorite porch chair, its back tilted against the wall. Now he let the chair drop with a thud, leaned forward, and shouted, "Go get it, girl! Reach for it!"

Candy stretched out and the ball settled on her fingertips. She pulled it in and raced for an imaginary goal line, brown hair flying, fist clenched high. She trotted back, grinning, toward the house. Her brother Casper, who usually answered to Cap, didn't smile back.

Grandpa Tully applauded. "Heck of a catch, Candy. Cap, I never saw an arm like yours on a boy your age. You can air it out."

Candy flipped the ball to her brother. She was fourteen, two years older than Cap. "Let's try a post pattern," she said. "I give the defender an inside move and go deep."

Cap rolled his eyes and groaned.

Candy ran in front of him, cutting him off. "Cap, c'mon, okay? I feel pumped!"

Cap shook his head. "Well, *I* don't. I feel flat. Let's call it a day."

Candy put a hand on her brother's arm. "Come on, just one more. It's late fourth quarter, we're down by four, and it's third and ten. It's now or never. Cap?"

Cap scowled but said nothing. Candy took his silence for agreement.

"All *right!*" She clapped her hands. "Set!" She bounced on her toes. Scowling, Cap held the football at his side.

"*Hut* one! *Hut* two!" Candy started fast, stopped short, head-faked right, and took off left.

Cap fired the ball as hard as he could. It sailed through the sky, yards out of Candy's reach. Not waiting to see where the ball went, he wheeled around and headed for the porch.

2

The girl glared at Cap. "Ha ha. What's eating you, anyway?" She trotted off to retrieve the ball.

Cap clomped up the porch steps, not saying a word. Grandpa frowned.

"Something bothering you, boy?"

Cap slumped down next to Tully.

"Yeah, I feel . . . it's not *fair,* that's all."

"What?" Grandpa studied Cap's face. "Must be bad, for you to treat your sister bad."

Cap looked at him and then down again. "That *was* dumb, I know. Well, you said it yourself. I have a great arm, I could be a great quarterback, but all I ever get to do is play pickup games or catch with Candy. I'll never be on a real team in a real game, and it isn't fair."

He heard Candy's footsteps on the porch steps and looked up. She was mad.

"Uh, sorry," he said. "That was a dopey thing to do. Guess I'm in a bad mood."

Candy fired the football at him, and Cap barely grabbed at it before it hit him in the chest. "That makes two of us. What's your problem?"

Grandpa said, "Cap wishes he could play on a real football team." He stopped and scratched his

3

head, thinking. "Come to think of it, why *couldn't* you?"

"Aw, you know, Grandpa." Cap stood and began pacing back and forth on the porch. "Cowpen is so small — what is it, two hundred and fifty people?"

"Two hundred and thirty-four," Candy said. "No, wait, Ms. Klinger had her baby last week. Two hundred and thirty-five."

"See?" Cap shook his head. "In our whole school, we have sixteen middle-grade boys. It's not enough for a team."

Tully nodded. "Not for an *eleven*-man team, but you could have a *six*-man team."

Cap laughed. "*Six-man* football? Six on a team? That's not real football."

"Oh, no?" Tully snatched the ball. "Let me tell you, when I was your age, all our schools played six-man football, in a league. And *I* was our quarterback, and team captain."

Cap and Candy exchanged glances. "That's great, Grandpa," Cap said, "but still, it wasn't . . . well . . . *real* football."

Tully Wadell's eyes flashed. "Oh, you mean like

with all those big hulks lumbering around like they have today? Ha! Our game was faster! We played offense *and* defense. *Real* football. Huh!"

"Why did they stop?" asked Candy.

Tully sighed. "Cowpen got too small to even get six on a side. But there're six-man leagues all over Texas, and other states, wherever the population is thin."

Cap found that he was getting interested about the possibility. *Could* it happen here?

"Grandpa, how would we start it up? You really think there's a chance we could?"

Tully grinned at his grandson. "Well, we could surely give it a try! I could —"

"Hey, Cap! What's happening?"

Cap's best friends, Hoot Coleman and Ben Worthy, rode their bikes into the Wadells' yard. Hoot was a wiry redhead, an inch shorter than the lanky Cap, and Ben was stocky with blond hair cut short. Both wore jerseys of their favorite football teams over faded jeans.

"Yo, Cap, how about a little ball?" asked Ben. "Hi, Candy, how you doing?"

Cap waved them over. "Guys, listen to this. How'd

you like to start a school football team? Maybe even a league?"

Ben snickered. "I'd like to go to the moon on a rocket but I won't do that either."

Hoot said, "Shoot, Cap, our school's too small. You'd need too many guys, and —"

"No," Cap said, "Grandpa's telling us about this six-man football the schools here used to play. Gramps was a quarterback."

"That's right," Tully agreed. "My last year, the Panthers were undefeated. Five and oh."

"Really, Mr. Wadell?" Hoot sat on the porch. "How did this game work?"

"We used an eighty-yard field," Grandpa said. "Three backs, three linemen, and *everybody* was an eligible receiver."

"Linemen could carry the ball?" asked Ben, who was built to be a lineman. "Cool!"

Grandpa nodded. "You needed fifteen yards for first down. A field goal was four points. After a touchdown, you got two for kicking a try and one for running or passing it in."

Ben looked puzzled. "How come you got two for a kick?"

6

Cap took a guess. "I bet there weren't many place-kickers, so kicking field goals and extra points deserved something extra."

Grandpa Tully patted Cap on the back. "Right. And I reckon we could put a league together in time for school this fall. If we can figure out how to get some uniforms . . ."

"Maybe local high schools can give us old ones," Ben said. "Pads and helmets, too."

"Tomorrow," said Tully, "I'll call Principal Vinson."

"Who's going to coach?" asked Candy.

Grandpa chuckled. "*Me!* The ex–star quarterback of the Cowpen Panthers!"

Cap beamed. "Great! I'll be quarterback, Hoot'll run, Ben can be a lineman, and —"

Tully held up his hands. "Whoa, slow down! Let's go one step at a time, all right?"

Cap saw that his friends were excited too. "You think this can work?" he asked Tully.

The man laughed. "I *know* it! You just wait . . . this fall, the Cowpen Panthers are *back!*"

2

A whistle sang out and eight Cowpen Panthers turned to their coach. Tully wore faded old sweats, and the boys had on gray practice jerseys and carried helmets.

Tully called, "Fellas, gather round."

Cap was amazed that it had happened so fast. Grandpa had called Principal Vinson, who thought six-man football was a great idea. He had spoken to other principals, and five schools — Sandville, Moosetown, Ausburg, Elmsford, and Bee Town — had organized teams of their own.

Tully and Mr. Vinson had contacted schools all over Texas and even some in Oklahoma. The schools had sent old uniforms and gear they no longer needed. The local schools had bought footballs and laid out fields that were eighty yards long and forty across.

In two weeks, the Cowpen Panthers would battle the Sandville 'Cudas in the first game of the season. Each team would play every other team in a five-game schedule.

Tully looked at the eight players and frowned. "Weren't there nine names on the bulletin board sign-up sheet?"

"Where's Jimmy Cash?" asked Sam Dracus, the fastest boy there and their probable deep threat. "His name was on the list."

"Well, he's late," said Tully. "Or he changed his mind."

Cap shook his head. "You mean this is all we're going to have? Eight guys?"

His grandfather replied, "All we need is six. Eight is enough, if we work at it."

"Well, but . . ." Cap looked at the little team. "How can we practice plays? We won't have a full offense *and* defense."

Tully shrugged. "We'll work it out. Meanwhile, let's do what we need to do first, which is learn how this game is played. Okay?"

The players all nodded, including Cap. But he couldn't see how the problem would be solved.

Other teams would have a big edge over Cowpen if they could field two squads for practice and the Panthers couldn't.

Tully smiled. "First, here are some ways this game is different from the one on TV. This is more wide open, there's more room for imaginative plays, and scores may be high. As far as passing goes, it's similar — except everyone can catch a pass.

"But you can't run the ball until the man who takes the snap makes a clear pass. That means a pass that goes back or sideways, a lateral. After that, you can run the ball. No handoffs, sneaks, or bootlegs, no runs *period,* until that clear pass. Breaking that rule costs you five yards *and* loss of down. Don't forget." Tully looked at the eight boys in front of him. "Now, have we got a placekicker?"

Hesitantly, Hoot raised his hand. "I can kick, a little. I tried a few times once and I actually put one between the goalposts, in three tries. But I'm not much good at it."

Tully grinned. "Work on your kicking fifteen minutes a day. A good kicker is valuable. Remember, in this game a field goal gets you four points. After a touchdown, you get one point when you run or pass, but *two* points if you kick it. So —"

"Hey," said a voice behind Tully. "Sorry we're late, Grandpa couldn't start the truck."

Tully turned and smiled at the new arrival, a tall boy with a shock of black hair. "You must be Jimmy Cash. Well, you haven't missed much, Jimmy, I've just been going over some rules."

"That's all right. *I* told Jimmy all about the rules last night. I still know 'em." The speaker was a lanky man with gray hair and a mustache who strolled up smiling.

Tully smiled too, but Cap didn't think there was pleasure in the smile. "Sable Cash."

Sable nodded. "I thought you boys could use a quarterback."

"Well, fine, Sable. Actually, *my* grandson, Cap here, is a quarterback, too. The boy has a rifle arm . . . like his granddad."

Sable chuckled as though he'd heard a good joke. "Yes, I recollect you *could* throw a fair pass back then . . . pretty near as good as me."

Tully's smile grew thin. "I recall that Cowpen was

11

undefeated our senior year, and Sandville finished second."

"Right. I broke my leg and couldn't play the last game against you, or it would've been different. Jimmy here is good. I hope you give him a fair chance — even if he isn't a relative."

Tully's face turned red. "Everybody will get a shot. Today's only our first practice."

Sable Cash looked unconvinced. "You need help with the coaching? I have some time." Cap saw Ben and Hoot exchange a look.

"I don't expect I'll need you, thanks." Tully's words were polite and his tone soft, but Cap knew Grandpa was steamed. He looked at Jimmy and caught the other boy staring at *him.* They both dropped their eyes.

"Hmph," grunted Sable, shaking his head. "Jimmy, I'll pick you up later and I want a full report of what you all did today. You hear?"

"Sure." Jimmy didn't look happy.

Tully watched Sable walk away and said, "Boys, give me a minute."

He walked after Sable, caught his arm, and the

two began to speak. Cap couldn't hear them but it didn't look like a friendly chat.

Hoot nudged Cap's arm. "Hey, Cap, *you're* going to be our quarterback, aren't you? Your grandpa's the coach, right?"

"Well . . ." Cap looked at Jimmy talking to Sam Dracus and Fritz Marconi, who was new in town and whom Cap didn't know. He didn't really know Jimmy either, except to say hi to. Just because there were only a few kids in school didn't mean everybody hung out with everybody else.

Cap felt confused and not sure what to say. Ever since the idea of six-man football had come up, he had just assumed that he'd be the quarterback. Grandpa was always talking about what a great passer he was, the best he'd ever seen. Now, though . . . maybe Jimmy Cash was a great passer too. What then?

"Grandpa will do what's right," he assured Hoot. He believed it too. He just hoped that "what's right" meant he'd be the starting quarterback.

3

Sable Cash drove off, raising a cloud of dust. Tully came slowly back to the team. He looked at each boy in turn, ending up with his eyes on Jimmy.

"Son, Sable says you can really throw the ball. And I guess he'd know."

Jimmy said, "Thank you, Mr. Wadell."

"Call me Coach. That goes for all of you. And I want this clear: Each of you will get the chance to show your stuff. No favorites. True, only six can start, but I guarantee you'll all get plenty of playing time. You play offense and defense, so I'll shuttle players in and out to keep you fresh. With two talented passers, we'll find ways to use you both. We might use you at the same time now and then and drive the opposition crazy. Any questions?"

No one had questions, and so practice began.

Tully taught them pass patterns: sideline routes where a receiver could turn upfield or step out of bounds to stop the clock, hooks, two-man patterns with one receiver going deep and another cutting over the middle. He showed a swing pass to a running back with linemen pulling to block downfield.

"Here's one for you, Ben," Tully said. "I don't suppose it's giving away secrets that you're going to be a center. Jimmy, come in for Cap and I'll explain. We scored against Bee Town with this in my playing days."

Ben snapped the ball to Jimmy and took a step back as if to block. Jimmy faked a pitchout to Vince at halfback, pump-faked to Sam going deep, and shoveled an underhand pass to Ben, who raced up the middle.

Tully grinned. "That'll still work, I bet."

He alternated between Jimmy and Cap at quarterback. Jimmy was good with timing patterns and short passing, but his arm wasn't up to throwing bombs; Cap saw that if Jimmy went long, he threw high floaters that anyone — receiver or defender —

could get to. Still, Cap couldn't deny that Jimmy was a good ball handler who could fake a lateral and fool defenses.

Cap, on the other hand, *could* throw deep, and Sam could outrun defenders — if Cap didn't overthrow him and Sam could hang on to the ball. Sam was the fastest Panther but didn't have the greatest hands. Fritz Marconi looked like a powerful runner, and his solid frame suggested that he'd be a good blocker.

Cap had played enough pickup ball with Hoot Coleman to know he was shifty, could fool tacklers, and put on a burst of speed when needed. Stocky Ben Worthy was a natural center, with surprisingly good hands. Once he saw Ben's ability to catch, Tully added a play in which Ben went out ten yards and hooked. Cap's pass was slightly behind Ben, who reached back with one hand and managed to pull the ball in.

The coach applauded. "All right! We're going to throw some in your direction, for sure."

Mick Avery, though he was short, had good moves and could catch everything coming his way. His younger brother Vince, though taller, was less coordinated, and likely to be a reserve. Steve Flynn wasn't very athletic, but he was enthusiastic, always talking it up and yelling encouragement. He'd be good to have around and might improve as a player.

"Cap!" called Tully. "Let's run Blue Streak Right again. Sam, go deep. Mick, go out eight yards and hook. Ben, drop back to block."

The players took positions. Cap called, "Blue Streak Right, on two! *Down! Set! Hut* one, *hut* two . . .*"

Cap dropped back three steps, pumped toward Mick, and fired downfield. Sam sprinted hard, but the ball was two feet beyond his reach. Disgusted with himself, Cap kicked the turf.

"It's okay, you'll nail it next time," Ben said, giving Cap a pat on the back. "It's just the first day."

Cap didn't feel better. He was in for a battle with Jimmy, who was looking very good.

Sam retrieved the ball and trotted back. He tossed the ball to Tully and grinned at Cap.

"I'll need a stepladder for those bombs."

Cap flushed. "Maybe you could just try hustling a little more."

Sam's grin vanished. "Don't blame me if you can't control the ball!"

Quickly, Tully stepped in. "I don't want to hear that stuff. Teammates work together."

Cap and Sam nodded. As Sam walked away, he whispered to Jimmy, who laughed. Tully frowned at his grandson.

"Sam didn't mean anything by that, he was kidding you."

Cap wished he could be sure. He had been looking forward to this day, but it wasn't working out the way he had hoped.

Tully worked on clear passes, using Mick and Fritz as running backs. He created an end-around play, with Cap or Jimmy faking a pitch to Fritz and tossing the ball to Sam, who came in from right end. Fritz and Mick would block. Jimmy looked better on pitchouts and laterals at first, but Cap quickly improved.

Cap's last pitchout was smooth.

"Lookin' good," said Jimmy.

Cap was startled. It was the first time Jimmy had spoken to him.

"Thanks," he replied. "If I'm lucky, I'll get it down as good as you have it now."

Tully whistled the team together. "I'm holding off

18

on defenses until tomorrow because it's hard to run them without an offense to practice against. I just figured out a way to work around our lack of players. I'll call the other coaches and see about scheduling scrimmages with other schools."

"But what'll we do till then?" asked Vince Avery.

Cap thought a moment. "Well, we —"

"Hey, Cap, Grandpa!" called a voice. "How's it going?"

Candy Wadell waved from the side of the field where she stood with her best friend, Bobby Jo Keller. Both girls were tall and athletic, and they joined in pickup games often. Seeing them gave Cap an idea.

"Gramps, maybe Candy and Bobby Jo could help us. You know, so we could work on our plays against a whole team, or close to it."

Sam Dracus's jaw dropped in disbelief. "Work out with *girls?* You serious?"

"You got any better ideas?" Cap demanded. "Candy is an athlete, she's fast, and that goes for Bobby Jo too. They can both catch passes as good as you, I bet."

"Oh yeah?" Sam snapped.

Tully held up a hand. "Cap may have an idea there."

"But —" Steve Flynn started to say.

"No, listen," said Tully. "This could solve our problem. Scrimmages are useful, if I can set them up, but if we get a practice squad to work with, we'll be better off. I know these girls, and Cap is right about them. They'll both play basketball for Cowpen next winter. I say if they're willing to help, let's be grateful for it."

"Makes sense to me," said Jimmy. Once again, Cap was surprised.

Fritz Marconi's face lit up. "I have an idea. My buddy Gabe Muñoz is in ninth grade now, so he's too old for our team, but he can play. I bet he'd join the practice squad. Then we'd have twelve players, so we could practice with two full teams."

"Hey, yeah," said Mick. "Gabe is good."

Tully nodded. "Fritz, give your friend a call." He beckoned to Candy and Bobby Jo and explained what he wanted. Both girls said they'd be happy to start coming to practice the next day.

Tully looked satisfied. "Well, if Gabe comes too, then we can really work. Tomorrow we go over what we did today and start learning some defensive —"

He was interrupted by a roaring engine and a squeal of brakes. Sable Cash's dusty pickup stopped by the field, and Sable hopped out. Cap heard Tully mutter something.

Sable nodded to Tully as he walked over but spoke only to his grandson. "So, Jimmy, did you get to throw?"

Cap thought that Jimmy looked uncomfortable. "Sure, Gramps. Coach had us taking turns."

Sable gave Tully a sharp glance and turned back to Jimmy. "Really?"

"You heard him," Tully said. "We're not finished, so why don't you —"

"You sure you wouldn't like some help?" Sable asked before Tully could finish.

Tully's smile was strained. "Like I told you, Sable, we're managing just fine."

Candy cleared her throat, sensing the tension between the men. "Grandpa, see you tomorrow, then."

"Thanks, hon, Bobby Jo."

Candy's friend ran a hand through her curly blond hair. "This'll be fun. Bye!"

Sable stared at the girls as they walked away. "What's *that* about? What are they looking forward to?" he asked Jimmy.

"They're going to practice with us starting tomorrow. That way, we —"

"Those *girls?*" Sable's jaw dropped. "Practicing with *you?*"

"It's really a good idea, Grandpa," Jimmy said, shooting a troubled glance at Tully. "See, we don't have enough guys to have a full offensive and defensive team, so —"

Sable snorted. "Now I've heard everything."

"Sable, we're not done," Tully said again. "Give us a few minutes, if you don't mind."

Sable studied Tully for a long moment. "You and I aren't done yet either, Wadell."

He walked slowly back to his truck. Looking over his shoulder, he called, "Jimmy, when the coach lets you go, I'll be waiting over here."

Cap and Jimmy looked at each other, but neither one spoke.

Cap wondered to himself whether Jimmy was feeling as embarrassed as he was.

4

The second day of practice, Tully had twelve players to work with. Candy and Bobby Jo were there, and Fritz's friend Gabe Muñoz. No one was wearing pads or helmets.

"Today, we'll add defenses and run plays," Tully explained. "Since we don't have enough equipment, we won't do any tackling."

He divided the group into two squads.

"This is to start with. We'll do some switching around later," Tully said. "Remember, this isn't a full-contact practice. You can block, but no hard tackles today."

He ran through the plays he had given the team so the newcomers could pick them up. When Tully saw everyone knew the plays, he said, "Time for defenses. Let's try a three-two-one defense."

He positioned Ben in the middle of the line with Fritz and Mick as defensive ends. He placed Hoot and Cap five yards back, with Sam five yards deeper.

"Sam, you're the safety," Tully explained. "If a play gets by you, it can mean six points for the opposition. Your job is to watch the play and go where the action is. If they send someone deep, you cover him."

He turned to the others. "You linemen should put pressure on the quarterback. Cap and Hoot, always watch the play develop. If it looks like a run, move in to stop it. Remember, no one can advance the ball by running until they throw a clear pass.

"Before each play, the defense should huddle like the offense and choose a coverage and who'll rush the quarterback. Keep the offense guessing about how many will be rushing the passer, and who. The key to defense is to stay alert and react. Always know where the ball is and keep your head in the game. If you just rush in blindly, the play may get by you before you know what's happening. Any questions?"

No one had any.

Tully smiled. "All right, defense, huddle up! I'll give the offense a play, and Cap, call a defensive pattern. Remember, the offense needs fifteen yards for a first down."

Jimmy had Candy and Vince at end, Gabe and Bobby Jo in the backfield, and Steve at center. Taking Steve's snap, he dropped back, looking for a receiver. Candy went deep and Sam picked her up. Steve blocked Ben, while Vince faked an inside move and cut to the sideline, fooling Cap, who went with the fake. Vince caught Jimmy's pass in full stride. Hoot ran Vince down after a twelve-yard gain.

Tully clapped his hands. "Good throw, Jimmy, and Vince, nice move on Cap! Cap, you see what happened there?"

Cap nodded. "Yeah, I got beat."

"Because you were too eager. You played Vince too tight off the line and didn't wait and react. Sam, you played off Candy a bit too much. If she'd pulled up, Jimmy could have thrown beneath you and she'd have been open."

Sam looked down at his feet.

"It's okay," Tully said. "This is new and you'll adjust. Each game, you'll have to learn the other guys' strengths and weaknesses as you play. Don't worry, you're doing fine! Now, it's second and three. Cap, set a defense."

Cap put two men on the line, with two linebackers playing outside the linemen. Sam and Hoot were deep, looking for a possible pass and to guard against a runner breaking away.

On the snap, Jimmy spun, faked a handoff to Gabe, and followed his block into the line. Tully's whistle stopped the play.

"That'll cost five yards and a down, Jimmy. You can't run without a clear pass."

Jimmy turned red. "Sorry, I just forgot."

Tully nodded. "Old habits die hard. Okay, go again. It's now third down and eight."

Cap left the defense as it was. Jimmy had his backs in an *I* formation. On the snap, Steve and Vince double-teamed Ben, shoving him to the right, while Gabe, the up back, charged Cap. Jimmy pitched to Bobby Jo, who ran left, but Cap spun away from Gabe and met Bobby Jo at the line of scrimmage.

"Good reaction!" Tully called. "You waited to see the play develop and then moved!"

After more plays, the squads switched roles, with

Cap's group going to offense. In the huddle, Cap called for a deep pass to Sam.

Three defenders rushed Cap. Ben held off Steve, and Hoot screened out Vince. Cap rolled away from Bobby Jo and fired toward Sam — but Candy, going step for step with the receiver, cut in front and picked it off.

Cap pounded his hands together in frustration as Candy trotted back, a big grin on her face. "Good pick, Candy," called Tully.

Sam said, "That girl can *run*."

Candy handed Cap the ball. "I knew you'd go deep. I was ready for it."

Tully nodded. "I had the same hunch. Cap, don't get predictable. If you rely on those bombs, they'll blow up in your face once the other team figures you out."

Cap had to admit that Tully had a point. There was more to learn in this game than he had expected.

5

During the next week, the team began to play together better, and everyone, even Sam, agreed that having extra people to work with — girls included — was helpful. Sable always drove Jimmy to practice and began staying to watch.

It was clear to Cap that Tully didn't welcome the other man's presence, although he wasn't in any position to do much about it. It was a free country, and Tully didn't want to embarrass the team members, especially Jimmy.

From the first day, everyone knew that Ben Worthy would start at center. Defensively, he was an intimidating pass rusher. By week's end, it was clear who most of the other starters would be.

Sam Dracus's speed made him a deep threat, and he would start at one end. When he raced out on a post pattern, the opposition would have to send someone deep, so even on a short pass or running play, the defense would be spread thinner. On defense, Sam would cover the other team's fastest receiver.

Mick Avery had nailed down the starting job at the other end. Mick always seemed to be able to get clear. He could also block well.

Hoot Coleman was a threat as a runner and pass receiver and would be a starting back. Fritz Marconi was a solid runner in short yardage situations and a strong lead blocker.

Vince Avery would be coming in as a running back and Steve Flynn could give Ben a breather at center or come in as an end.

But if Tully had decided who would start at quarterback, he wasn't saying. He kept alternating between Cap and Jimmy. Both boys had their strengths: Cap had a stronger arm and was a better defender than Jimmy and a good blocker. But he tended to go deep too often, and his short passes were often thrown so hard that they were tough for his receivers to hang on to.

Jimmy's short passing game was his strength. He

was a smart play caller and more ready to use all the weapons at his disposal. But he couldn't throw long passes well, and wasn't as good as Cap on defense.

When Cap compared himself with Jimmy, he had to admit that Tully had a tough choice to make. It wasn't made easier by Sable's being around. If Tully went with Cap, Sable would make noise about it. And Cap knew that if Tully picked Jimmy as the starter, Tully would be unhappy because Cap would be unhappy.

The next day, when no one was near enough to hear him except Tully and Candy, he said, "Uh, Grandpa, I wanted to tell you . . ."

He stopped, unsure of what to say.

"What, son?" asked Tully.

"I just want to say . . . Jimmy's a good quarterback too, and . . . if you think he should start, that's all right."

Tully put a hand on his shoulder. "I appreciate you telling me that, Cap."

"Well, I think Cap should start," Candy said. "He's a better player than Jimmy any day."

Cap smiled gratefully at his sister. "I don't know. Jimmy's good."

Tully pointed to where the rest of the team stood waiting. "Let's get started. I have some news for everybody."

Cap noticed that Sable was with Jimmy and the other Panthers. He had stayed for all of yesterday's practice but had not said much.

Tully said, "First, we have a scrimmage scheduled next Tuesday with Bee Town. We're due there at four. If you can get rides from your folks, that'd be helpful."

"I can help with that," said Sable.

Tully nodded. "Thanks."

"How does the scrimmage work?" Sam asked.

"It's played under game rules, on a regulation field," Tully said. "Each team runs a certain number of plays and then we switch. We'll have full pads and helmets, thanks to some last-minute donations we're due to receive tomorrow morning. We won't keep score, because even though we play by official rules, it's just a kind of practice. In the next few days, we need to work on special team stuff: kickoffs, receiving, and punts. Also, extra-point plays —"

Sable cleared his throat. "Tully, you don't mind my hanging around, do you?"

"Be my guest," Tully replied.

They practiced the plays they had been working on, with Jimmy and Cap alternating at quarterback, and Candy, Bobby Jo, and Gabe filling out the practice squad.

At one point, Cap called a pitch to Hoot, going around left end with Fritz clearing away tacklers. Ben snapped and pulled to his left, Fritz thundering by his side. Cap pivoted and Hoot broke left. Cap flipped the ball behind Hoot's back and kicked the ground angrily as Tully whistled the play dead.

"Sorry," Cap said to Hoot, who shrugged. "We'll get 'em next time."

Jimmy wouldn't have done that, Cap thought. Maybe he deserves to be the starter.

Sable strolled over. "Son, you mind a suggestion from an old fossil?" He turned to Tully. "If it's okay with you, that is."

Tully nodded.

Sable picked up the football. "The reason you have trouble controlling a pitchout is partly footwork. Take a longer first step so your feet aren't too close together. When you pitch the ball, make more of a full-arm motion, not a wrist flip. 'Specially since your hands aren't big enough to control the ball all that well."

Sable looked at Hoot. "Make that move again, son, and I'll show you all how it's done."

Hoot took off as he had done for Cap, and Sable gracefully wheeled around and made a perfect pitch, which Hoot caught in full stride.

Cap had to admit it did look better than his clumsy move.

"Now you try it," said Sable, taking the ball from Hoot and giving it to Cap.

This time, Cap tried to do exactly what Sable had done and found that it made a difference. The ball was right on target.

"There you go," said Sable.

"Thanks, Mr. Cash," Cap said.

Sable grinned. "Jimmy makes pitchouts well because I taught him what I just taught you. Pitchouts are important in this game, wouldn't you say, Tully?"

"Uh-huh," Tully said.

Sable picked up another ball. "Listen, long as I'm going to be around anyway, why not let me help? I mean, you have your hands full with everything these fellas still have to learn, and I can split things up with you. What do you say?"

Tully's jaw muscles were clenched, and it was clear to Cap that his grandfather wasn't delighted by the idea.

Sable held up a hand before Tully could reply. "Now, I understand this is still your team. I'd be just an assistant."

Finally Tully said, "That would be fine with me, Sable. I guess it may be a little too much for one man, at that."

Sable chuckled. "That's the idea! And, after all, pitchouts and ball handling were never specialities of yours in our playing days, were they?"

Cap saw Jimmy turn away, red-faced.

6

Tully ran practice that day, as usual. But now that Tully had accepted him as an assistant, Sable seemed to feel he had the right to comment on everything the Panthers did.

Sometimes it would be about Tully's choice of strategy: "You better hope Sandville doesn't have any audibles to call at the line, or they'll read that defense, change plays, and short-pass you to death, with the middle open like that."

Sometimes it would be about the way a player carried out an assignment. Many of these comments were aimed at Cap, and they were always just loud enough for Cap to hear: "The boy just loves those bombs. As soon as a defense reads that tendency, they'll send in rushers, hurry the passes or play soft

35

against sweeps and short gains, and look for the bomb."

The one he never criticized was Jimmy.

Then, just when Tully was about to explode, Sable would give some good advice. After Candy beat Sam and caught a sideline pass from Jimmy, Sable went to the unhappy boy. "Sam, if you drop back three more yards as she comes off the line and watch her belt buckle, you can anticipate her cut. A receiver can fake with his head or with his feet, but he can't fake with the middle of his body."

Which, Cap saw, was valuable advice.

Even with the tension it was a good practice, and Cap saw that the Panthers were beginning to jell as a team and become familiar with the techniques of six-man football.

The happiest moment of the day came when Hoot tried to kick field goals through a pair of makeshift goalposts that Tully had had put up. Cap and Jimmy took turns as the holder.

Hoot's first try, from twenty yards away, flew way off to the right. He was kicking the old-fashioned way, approaching the ball straight on rather than soccer-style, from the side.

"Don't look up before you kick," Tully said. "I guarantee you, the goalposts won't move. Look at where you want the ball to go before the snap, then keep your head down. Don't worry about rushers — your blockers will keep them away, so don't get distracted."

Hoot's next kick sailed through the uprights, with yards to spare.

Tully and Sable clapped and the others cheered.

"Way to go!" Tully shouted. "Want to try moving the ball back a little?"

Hoot kicked one of two attempts from about the fifteen-yard line and was nearly automatic from point-after range.

"Keep working on the kicks," Sable said, "and you might add five or ten yards to your range. Those placekicks are valuable."

Hoot was good on kickoffs too, but the best punter on the team was Cap. He could sail a punt high so that defenders could reach a receiver quickly.

After working for a while on kickoffs, punts, and returns, Tully blew his whistle.

"Good work today, everyone! Cap, having a

quarterback who can punt means we might be able to try quick kicks sometime and catch 'em unawares. You can pick up a lot of yards with a quick kick."

Cap suddenly felt a rush of excitement. Did that mean he was going to be the starter?

"If your offense moves the ball the way it ought to," muttered Sable, "you shouldn't need to quick kick."

Tully didn't say anything in reply.

"See everyone here tomorrow at the usual time, ready to work!" Tully called. "We have two practices left before the scrimmage in Bee Town, so let's make the most of them."

"Hey, guys," called Ben, "who's up for going over to the Spot for something to eat?"

The Spot was Cowpen's snack shop and diner, and the main hangout for local kids.

"Cool!" Mick Avery said.

Several other players sounded eager to go, and Bobby Jo cleared her throat.

"Are practice squadders welcome too?"

"Sure," Sam said, grinning. "You guys are part of this team!"

Jimmy was smiling happily and looked over at

Sable. "Gramps, okay if I go? Someone can drop me off later."

Cap nodded. "We can give Jimmy a ride, right, Grandpa?"

"No problem," replied Tully.

Sable shook his head. "I think you'll have to take a rain check on that, Jim."

His grandson's face fell. "But —"

"You have chores to do at home," Sable explained. "There'll be other times."

"Okay," Jimmy mumbled, not looking at the other players.

Cap and Ben exchanged a glance, both feeling sorry for Jimmy.

"Sam, I'm supposed to drop you off at home, too," Sable added. "I had strict orders from your mom."

"Uh, maybe I should get home too," Fritz said.

"Well, I'm going, for sure," Hoot said.

The group at the Spot included six of the nine Panthers and the three practice-squad members as well. But there was a little cloud over the gathering.

Afterward, Hoot and Ben stood with Cap before heading home.

"Why'd Mr. Cash have to do that?" Ben asked, looking angry. "It wasn't right! Jimmy wanted to come with us."

"He surely did," Cap agreed. "And so did Sam, and I bet Fritz would have come too, if they had."

"Cap, what's the deal with Mr. Cash and your grandpa?" Hoot asked.

Cap shrugged. "Beats me. I know they used to play against each other a million years ago. It sounds like Mr. Cash still has it in for Grandpa, even now."

"Your grandpa is a nice man," Ben said. "But, you know, he doesn't exactly love Mr. Cash, either."

Cap nodded wearily. "Guess he doesn't. I don't get it — all this about some old games from way back! I hope they can get over it."

"Me, too," Hoot agreed. "They're our coaches, and we're a team. They have to work together."

Cap sighed. "Maybe I'll talk to Grandpa tonight and ask him whether he and Mr. Cash can get along better. We have enough to worry about without our coaches getting on each other like that."

"Good idea," Hoot said. "Could be they don't re- alize that it's making the rest of us uncomfortable."

"Yeah, and it could hurt the team," Ben added.

"Well, I'll sure give it a shot," Cap answered.

But in his own mind he was asking himself, If Grandpa picks me to start, are he and Mr. Cash going to have a war?

7

After dinner, Candy went inside to help their father do the dishes. Their mother went upstairs to work at her computer. Tully was relaxing on his favorite porch chair and Cap figured this was a good time to bring up the tricky subject. He sat next to his grandfather on a footstool.

"We're looking pretty good, huh, Grandpa?"

Tully tilted his chair against the wall.

"You're making good progress. It'd be nice if we had two more weeks, but then again, none of the other teams has any more time than we do."

Cap thought about what to say next. "So, you and Mr. Cash go back a long way, I guess."

Tully sighed. "In our high school days, he and I were the stars our senior year. Cowpen and Sandville, where he played, were the two best teams. Yes, we go a ways back."

"But Cowpen was the champ, right?"

Tully nodded. "We were undefeated that year and beat Sandville after they'd been undefeated too. Course, Sable couldn't play, because he'd broken his leg, but I believe we'd have beaten them anyway, just not as bad."

"Huh," Cap said, and thought a moment. Then, just loud enough for Tully to hear, he went on. "I guess that explains it, then."

"Explains what?"

"Well, you and he aren't exactly best friends, Grandpa. I guess it's because he still thinks about not being able to play in that game and losing the championship to your team."

"I guess it bothers him," Tully replied. "Although why, after all these years, is a mystery to me."

"Grandpa, do you like Mr. Cash?"

Tully let his chair down.

"Like him? Why do you ask?"

"The two of you rub each other the wrong way. I mean, I understand him being sore about what happened back then, but you won the game. How come you're sore at him?"

Tully frowned. "Now, hold on a minute, boy. Who says I'm sore at him? I have nothing against Sable Cash. Nothing. Except . . . well, except he makes all these digs at me and tries to cut me down as a coach in front of you boys, which does get to me a little. You can understand that, can't you?"

"Sure I can," Cap said quickly. "But —"

"And Sable wants Jimmy to be the starting quarterback, which is my decision to make, not his. And he keeps going on about it, and I don't like that, either."

Cap nodded. "Jimmy's good."

"Sure he is, son, but so are you. I won't deny it's a hard choice. But whichever one of you starts, you'll both get plenty of playing time. Thing is, if I pick you, I know Sable will tell everyone I did it because you're family, and I really don't like that."

"Sure, I can see that," Cap answered. "I just . . . I wish there was a way to . . . sort of straighten things out between you and Mr. Cash so the two of you could be friends. Or maybe not friends, but at least so you wouldn't get on each other's nerves as much."

Tully's frown got darker. "Casper Wadell, you stop right there. You're talking to the wrong man. If you want to straighten this out, then you have a word with Sable Cash, because this is all his doing and none of mine. Is that clear?"

Cap felt miserable. "But I can't talk to Mr. Cash about this, Grandpa. It's not my place to —"

"Well, I don't want to talk about it with you either. Like I said, it's Sable's problem and it's up to him to take care of it. Good night."

Tully stood up and walked quickly inside.

Great, Cap thought. I probably just made things even worse.

Candy came outside. "Hey, bro, what's up? I just saw Grandpa marching through the living room, looking like he was going to bust. You guys have a fight?"

Cap sighed and sat on the porch steps. "I tried talking to him about Mr. Cash, and he didn't like it."

"Oh. That." Candy sat next to her brother. "Yeah, those two don't get along, do they."

"It's bad for the team," Cap said. "They're both supposed to be helping us, but they're always sniping at each other, especially Mr. Cash, but Grandpa

45

too. Yesterday, when Mr. Cash wouldn't let Jimmy or Sam go to the Spot with the rest of us, it was . . . Everybody felt bad, especially Jimmy. He's a nice guy, and I — what can we do about it?"

Candy nodded. "Bobby Jo and I were talking about it yesterday. You have a problem, for sure, and I'm surprised at Grandpa. I'd never have thought he'd get into a feud, like a little kid. I wish I could tell you I had an idea what to do, but the truth is, I don't have a clue. Bobby Jo is real good about talking to people but she didn't have any ideas either. She says that when grown-ups start behaving like kids, they don't want kids telling them about it."

"Guess she's right. Grandpa nearly bit my head off. What I don't get is it's all about stuff that happened even before our parents were born," Cap said.

"Grown-ups can be weird sometimes," Candy replied. "Hopefully they'll work it out themselves. They must see that it makes all of you guys uncomfortable."

"Sure they do," Cap said, "and I bet each of them thinks it's the other one's fault." He looked at his sister and shook his head. "When Grandpa came up with this idea of six-man football, I was pumped! I was totally looking forward to it."

Candy gave Cap a look of sympathy. "Guess nothing is ever as simple as you hope it'll be. But I still think everything'll work out all right. Mr. Cash and Grandpa are good people, after all."

Cap nodded agreement. "Sure they are. They're good people who don't like each other much."

8

A little fleet of vehicles from Cowpen pulled into the Bee Town school parking lot on the afternoon of the scrimmage. Tully had driven his station wagon, Sable Cash had his pickup, and Clete Avery, Mick and Vince's father, had driven too. They had taken the whole Panther team, including the practice squad. Even though Candy, Bobby Jo, and Gabe would not be able to play in the scrimmage, they wanted to be there.

In their blue-and-gold uniforms and carrying their spikes, the team walked around the school to where the eighty-yard field had been freshly painted. A sign saying HOME OF THE BEE TOWN COBRAS stood by the bleachers, and a man in a sweat suit came forward.

"Tully Wadell?" he asked, smiling.

Tully stepped forward. "That's me."

"Pleased to meet you. I'm Cal Van Dyke, the Bee Town coach, and our boys will be out in a minute."

Sable Cash cleared his throat.

"Cal, this is Sable Cash, who's been, uh, helping me get our team ready."

As they all shook hands, another man came out of the school building and joined them.

Cal nodded to the newcomer and explained, "Baird Hoskins, one of our teachers, has agreed to be referee today. He grew up listening to his dad talk about six-man ball, so he knows the rules. Plus he's officiated at high school games."

"We appreciate your help," said Tully.

"My pleasure," said Hoskins, who wore a white cap and T-shirt and carried a whistle and stopwatch. "I'm glad to see this game back."

"Here they come," Cal said, gesturing with a thumb toward the school building. Twelve boys in gray uniforms with red trim trotted toward them, spikes clattering on the pavement.

Cap thought they seemed older. Then he decided

it was because they were in uniforms and pads. But there was no denying that Bee Town had *twelve* players to Cowpen's nine.

Would it matter? Cap wasn't sure. Maybe, on a hot day, the team with more players could stay fresher, but the thing to remember was that nine *good* players would beat twelve not-so-good players — and nine *well-coached* players would beat twelve that weren't as well coached.

But what about a team with *two* coaches who were always getting on each other's nerves? And the nerves of their players, as well?

Tully and Cal introduced their players to the other team. As each player's name was given, the player stepped forward. When Cal Van Dyke called, "Vernon Dewey," a tall, skinny boy waved a hand, and Hoot nudged Cap's arm.

"I know Vernon," Hoot whispered. "He's a friend of my cousin's and I used to play with him when I was little. He couldn't put one foot in front of the other without tripping. If he's playing for Bee Town, we'll whip these guys."

Cap felt nervous. Tully had said he'd name his starters before the scrimmage began but that the players who started today weren't necessarily those who'd start the first real game.

After the players from both teams shook their opponents' hands, Baird Hoskins whistled for everyone's attention.

"Most regular rules will apply today. But we won't keep score. The team that wins the coin toss will run fifteen plays. If they score during those plays, they get the ball at their thirty-five-yard line and go until they've run their fifteen. If they lose the ball by fumble or interception, they play from the same line of scrimmage.

"After their fifteen, the other team goes on offense. If we have time, we'll do it again. Coaches can substitute as often as they want. Captains, step forward for the coin toss."

Two Bee Town players came forward, but none of the Panthers moved. Tully hadn't picked captains yet. The Cowpen players looked at him. So did Sable.

Tully said, "Cap, Jimmy, you're our captains today."

The ref flipped the coin, Cap called, "Heads," and the coin landed heads up.

Jimmy said, "We'll start on offense."

"All right," said Van Dyke. "We'll start in two minutes. Good luck, everyone."

As the Panthers gathered around Tully and Sable, Tully darted a glance at Sable before he spoke. "Listen up. Here are my starters. Ben at center, Sam and Mick at end, Fritz and Hoot at running back, and Cap at quarterback."

Cap heard Sable snort. He felt edgy.

"All right," Tully said, "let's see what we can do. I'll send in substitutes every few plays and sometimes they'll bring in a play to run. Otherwise, Cap and Jimmy — let's see how you call a game. Sable, anything to add?"

Sable said, "Boys, there may be more of these Bee Town fellows than us, but they can only put six on the field at once. Try to get an idea what their strengths and weaknesses are, and take advantage of the weaknesses. Use your heads as well as your bodies and play your best."

The referee blew his whistle and Cap trotted onto the field, feeling a rush of panic. He couldn't remember any plays! He'd mess everything up and look awful! Let Jimmy start!

Ben grinned at him, then took a closer look and asked, "You okay?"

Taking a breath, Cap muttered, "Yeah."

"Listen, I'm nervous too," Ben said. "We *all* are. Hey, we're ready. As soon as I snap that ball, you'll know what to do."

Cap felt himself relax and smiled gratefully at Ben. "Thanks. Let's get 'em."

Cap clapped his hands and the Panthers grouped around him. He took a quick glance at the Bee Town defense, but it told him nothing. He decided to open with a short pass.

"Red Flare Left on two!" he said and clapped again. The Panthers moved to the line.

The Cobras, Cap saw, had a man right over Ben and had set two defenders into the secondary. He felt sure that Ben could take care of the guy opposite him and thought the Cobras might give up some yardage over the middle.

"Hut one! Hut two!"

Ben snapped the ball, and as Cap dropped back he saw Ben slam a shoulder into the guy facing him, driving him backward. A second defender charged into the backfield but Fritz picked him up. Mick ran

53

downfield eight yards and cut sharply toward the sidelines, while Sam sprinted on a diagonal route over the middle.

Looking right and pumping the ball in Mick's direction, Cap saw Sam was open and fired a bullet toward him. Sam caught the ball and turned downfield, adding five yards to the seven gained on the pass before he was dragged down by two Cobras. Cap heard his sister and Bobby Jo cheering from the bleachers.

"Huddle up, Panthers!" Ben shouted.

Looking at his teammates, Cap felt totally in control. "Okay, Sweep Punch Veer on one! Break!"

This was a running play, with Ben and Fritz leading interference as Hoot went around left end. Sam would go deep to try to decoy some Cobras.

With the snap, Ben pulled to his left, and Fritz wheeled after him. Cap pivoted and lateraled perfectly to Hoot. Hoot swung in behind his blockers and got cut down by a pursuer who appeared from Cap's right.

This time the Cobra bench cheered after the Panthers' three-yard loss. Cap realized that the tackler had been *his* responsibility. But he had just stood there, watching the play develop.

He suddenly felt embarrassed and looked over to the sidelines, where he noticed Sable Cash saying something to Tully and pointing toward the field. Pointing at him, Cap thought, making sure that Tully knew Cap had messed up the play. He wanted to show them that he could do the job, but *how?*

Get six quick points, that was how.

Before he could call another play, Vince Avery ran in from the sidelines to replace Hoot.

"The coach has a play he wants us to run," said Vince.

Cap heard the play and groaned to himself. It was a running play. He wanted to go long, but his grandfather would be really hot if he didn't follow orders.

The play called for Cap to drop back as if to pass and flip a lateral to Fritz, who was set to his side as a flanker. Ben, Vince, and Cap would block while the ends ran a pattern to decoy the defense.

Sure enough, two Cobra defenders raced back to cover the pass that never came while Ben and Vince laid solid blocks to clear a path for Fritz. This time

Cap stayed alert, and when another Cobra tried to cut across and tackle the runner, Cap hit him low and brought the man down. Fritz picked up ten yards. Gabe, Candy, and Bobby Jo yelled encouragement and Tully had a big grin on his face.

Vince stayed in the lineup and Cap called for the long pass. He found himself running for his life as a Cobra got through Vince's block and chased him to his right. He saw that Sam had a step on his man, stopped, and unleashed a perfect spiral. Running flat out, Sam made a desperate dive, but the ball was a foot out of his reach.

Cap noticed that the Cobra who had covered Sam Dracus, and almost matched him step for step, was Vernon Dewey. He was probably their deep threat on offense, as well as a good pass defender. As Sam trotted back to the huddle, Cap said, "Sorry, that would have been six if it'd been just a bit shorter."

He was thinking about what he'd call next when he felt a tap on his shoulder, turned, and saw Jimmy standing there.

"Coach wants me in," said the other boy.

Cap nodded wordlessly and ran off the field. He only let me run four plays, that's not fair, he thought.

When he got to the sidelines, he thought Tully might explain, but his grandfather said nothing, just patted his shoulder and kept his eyes on the field. Sable Cash ignored him completely.

Candy came over and said, "You looked pretty good in there."

Cap snorted. "Yeah? Then how come I'm over *here?* After four plays!"

"Well . . ." Candy hesitated. "Maybe it was calling the long pass. I know Mr. Cash gave Grandpa an earful about it."

On the field, Jimmy tried a short sideline pass that Mick caught for a six-yard gain. Steve Flynn went in for Fritz and caught an eight-yard pass out of the backfield.

"Way to go, boy!" boomed Sable Cash. "He's making good play selections," he said to Tully. "He's got a quarterback's mind."

Tully nodded and leaned closer to Cap. "Sable has a point, son. Jimmy's good at mixing his calls, and you still have to remember that those long bombs aren't the kind of play you can call too often. They can really destroy a team's momentum."

Sure enough, Jimmy picked up another twelve

yards on his next two plays: a pass play to Ben at center, with Ben carrying two tacklers ahead for four yards, and a run by Vince around right end, with Hoot making a great block.

But on his next play, Jimmy's pitchout was wild, and Hoot couldn't reach it before a Cobra defensive player fell on the ball.

Jimmy glanced over at the sidelines, clearly upset, and Tully clapped and hollered, "It's all right, don't let it get to you!"

After Jimmy gained six yards with a pass over the middle, Tully sent Cap and Fritz back in. "You have four more plays," he told Cap, "make 'em count!"

On the next play, Cap hit Mick with a down-and-out pattern for ten yards, putting the Panthers on the Cobra ten-yard line. He sent Sam into the corner of the end zone and Mick to the other side of the field, then shoveled an underhand pass to Ben. Ben plowed straight ahead for six yards to the four. A running play, Fritz carrying up the middle with Cap making a block, picked up only one yard.

Cap had one more play and wanted to score *now*. He sent three receivers into the end zone, but as he looked the field over, there were Cobras too close to all of them to risk a pass. On the other hand, there was nobody on the line.

Cap flipped the ball to Fritz, who was back to block, then slammed into the first Cobra defender to get close. Fritz lowered his head and bulled forward, carrying the ball over the goal line.

The referee held his hands straight up, signifying a touchdown, and the other Panthers surrounded Fritz, cheering and pounding him on the back.

Cap had made the four plays count, he had called the plays that brought the Panthers their first touchdown. Sure, it was only a scrimmage, but he felt good about it anyway. And, he thought, maybe even Mr. Cash would be impressed. He, Cap, could play this game too.

Baird Hoskins blew his whistle. "Take two minutes, and Bee Town goes on offense."

On the sidelines, the Panthers milled around, giving each other high fives, feeling good. The practice squadders joined in until Tully called for everyone's attention.

"Let's not celebrate too soon," he said. "Time to show what we can do defensively. I'm going to start the same team as on offense and I'll substitute a lot so you'll get playing time. Remember, you play defense with your eyes and brains too. Stay alert, know where the ball is, and never forget your job on every play. Don't try to be a hero and do it all yourself."

"Right!" Sable Cash agreed. "If you're on the line of scrimmage, make sure you don't get faked out of position, don't leave big holes to run through. If you're on a receiver, look for feints and don't get beaten deep. *Talk to each other!* Don't get your signals crossed."

As they ran on the field, Cap said to Sam, "Watch out for the tall blond guy, Vernon, I think his name is. He can *fly.*"

Sam nodded. "He was covering me before. I'll give him room but not *too* much."

As the Cobras came to the line of scrimmage, their quarterback looked at the Panther defense, which wasn't giving him any clues. They had Ben and Fritz on the line, on either side of the center. Hoot and Mick were the linebackers, a few yards deep, with Sam and Cap in the secondary.

As the ball was snapped, Cap stayed in place and saw a receiver break toward him. He held back until he saw the quarterback flip a lateral to a running back and realized the end coming at him was a blocker. The Cobra lunged but Cap shoved him aside and ran to his left, in the direction of the play. He saw Ben double-teamed and Fritz chasing the runner from behind. Hoot got a hand on the runner's arm and slowed him down. Cap hurled himself forward and dragged the man down after a three-yard gain.

Sam patted Cap on the back. "Way to hustle!"

On the next play, the quarterback dropped back. Ben put pressure on him, and Cap saw Sam going deep, covering speedy Vernon Dewey. His man raced toward him, stopped abruptly, and pivoted toward the center of the field. Cap reacted quickly, but the receiver was open for a second, long enough for the passer to hit him with a bullet pass. Cap slammed into the man, but the pass was good for eight yards.

There was cheering from a handful of rooters in the bleachers. Cap stood up and brushed himself off. Hoot grinned at him.

"Good recovery, man. You dropped him before he could turn it into a big gain."

On the next play, the Panthers stonewalled an attempted run up the middle, with Ben plugging the hole and making the first hit and Mick and Fritz finishing it off.

Between plays, Sam whispered to Cap, "Watch for a pass. I have a hunch."

Sam and Cap dropped back a few steps as the Cobras came to the line. Cap saw that Vernon Dewey was on his side of the field.

"Don't let him get behind you," Sam called. "I'll help if I'm not too busy over here."

On the snap, Vernon turned on the afterburners and sprinted straight toward Cap. Cap backpedaled, then pivoted and ran as hard as he could, trying to stay between the receiver and the goal line. Out of the corner of his eye, he saw Sam racing hard, looking to help out.

The ball soared toward Vernon, who saw it at the same time Cap did. Both tried to get under it. Incredibly, the Cobra put on an extra burst of speed and got a step on Cap, who thought for a second that Vernon would make the catch. But a hurtling figure in blue and gold launched itself at the ball and tipped it with one outstretched hand. Sam crashed to the ground and Vernon made a grab for the ball, but Sam had deflected it so that it hit the ground, incomplete.

Cap helped pull Sam to his feet. "What a play! You saved six points, for sure."

Sam stood up and brushed himself off. "I thought Hoot said this guy was helpless."

Cap chuckled. "Now we know better."

The Cobras stayed away from long passes, but their short passing game, mixed in with a few runs, got them good yardage. On their ninth play they scored a touchdown. Cap was on the sidelines at the time, replaced by Jimmy two plays before.

Jimmy was a good tackler and played well against the run, but he wasn't as good at covering receivers as Cap. Vernon beat him badly on one pass play, faking him and getting past him for a twenty-yard run after a catch.

Cap overheard Sable mutter, "I *told* that boy to watch out. That skinny kid has good moves." Sable went to Tully. "We ought to double-team that kid on pass plays."

Tully shook his head. "We double-team him and we leave someone open. Maybe I'd do it in a game situation, but not here."

"You're the coach," snapped Sable, clearly not happy about the fact.

Jimmy subbed back in moments later. On their next-to-last play, the Cobras pulled a stunt play, with the quarterback lateraling to a halfback. Then, as the Panther defense rushed in to stop the run, the halfback pitched back to the quarterback. Cap looked over his shoulder to see a Cobra end, all alone, going deep. He took off after the receiver, knowing he wouldn't catch him in time.

The pass, however, was underthrown, forcing the end to wait for it and allowing Cap to make a touchdown-saving tackle. The Cobras were now twelve yards from the end zone and called a pass play, but Cap and Sam had both deep receivers tightly covered.

A safety-valve pass to a halfback was complete but Hoot and Steve brought the runner down six yards short of a score.

The unofficial score was tied.

The ref called both coaches over to confer and then announced, "We have time for each team to run six plays. Let's take five minutes and then it'll be Cowpen on offense."

Tully got the Panthers together. "Let's see if we can score again. Play as if we were in the last two minutes of a tie game." He paused for a moment. "Jimmy, you start, and the rest of the starting lineup is Hoot, Fritz, Mick, Ben, and Sam. We have six plays, so make 'em count!"

Cap called out encouragement to his teammates, hoping he didn't look as bothered by Tully's decision as he felt. Sable grabbed Jimmy by the arm and whispered a few last words before the teams took the field. Tully came over to Cap.

"Now don't worry — I'll send you in."

Cap smiled as convincingly as he could. He thought that he had played as well as Jimmy — better on defense, for sure.

Candy must have noticed that Cap wasn't happy. She and Bobby Jo joined Cap. Candy punched her brother lightly on the shoulder.

"You're still the man," she said, "and everyone here knows it, except for Mr. Cash, I guess. Don't let it get you down, bro."

Jimmy's first play was a short pass to Hoot that got the Panthers five yards.

"See?" Candy whispered to Cap. "*Too* short. That's a good play if you want to eat up the clock, but that's not what we need to do now."

"Right," said Bobby Jo. "We need a big play, and you're the big-play man."

Cap felt better.

Jimmy's next two plays, a run and another short

pass, gained a total of ten more yards. Tully beckoned to Cap.

"Go in and open it up," he ordered.

Cap saw Sable Cash scowling in the background as he ran on and gathered the team together. The Panthers were forty yards from a touchdown and had three plays.

He started with an underhand shovel pass to Ben at center, using his wide receivers to draw the secondary deep and out of position. Ben powered ahead, carrying a Cobra tackler the last few yards, and picking up twelve.

Cap then called a deep sideline pass, throwing to Mick for another fifteen yards and putting the Panthers on the thirteen-yard line.

He sent Mick into the left corner of the end zone. Sam put on a burst of speed that forced his defender to accelerate to keep up. But Sam hooked in toward the goalposts, getting free for Cap's pass. Cap's throw was high, but Sam leapt up to bring it down.

Touchdown, Panthers! Cap wasn't pleased with his accuracy but celebrated with his teammates anyway.

With the Panthers on defense, Cap stayed in the

game for the first three plays, during which they held Bee Town to only twelve yards. It seemed like they would keep the Cobras from scoring.

However, Tully sent in Jimmy, Steve, and Vince for Cap, Hoot, and Sam, and things suddenly changed. Steve blew an open-field tackle on a Cobra runner that allowed the runner to gain fifteen yards. On the next play, Vernon Dewey took off downfield, covered by Jimmy.

"Uh-oh," Sam muttered, just loud enough for Cap to hear. "Jimmy can't keep up with that guy."

Sure enough, Vernon sailed past Jimmy, who could only watch as Dewey caught the well-thrown pass in full stride and trotted over the goal line for six points.

Cap turned to Hoot, who was watching with his mouth hanging open.

"Great scouting report you gave us on that guy Dewey."

Hoot shrugged. "What can I say? He *used* to be helpless."

Candy leaned in over Cap's shoulder. "If Grandpa had left you and Sam in, they'd never have scored."

Recalling how Vernon had beaten him a while before, Cap replied, "Don't be so sure of that. Anyway, this is a scrimmage, and Grandpa needed to see what we could do — *all* of us."

But in his own mind he agreed with Candy that all in all he was the better of the two quarterbacks.

The two teams came together to shake hands and congratulate each other. As Vernon Dewey shook Cap's hand, Hoot stepped between the two and faced the gangly blond boy.

"Great game! Hey, you used to play with us when you were little, remember? You were pretty bad."

Vernon smiled. "Yeah, I guess I was, wasn't I."

"Not anymore," said Cap. "You almost beat us single-handed."

"We *would've* beat you, except that fellow Sam can really motor. Good game, guys."

"Panthers, let's head home," called Tully. "Good work, everybody. See you tomorrow afternoon — and be ready to work."

10

Tully," said Sable Cash, cutting Tully off on the way to the station wagon. "We need to talk. How about tonight?"

Tully nodded, not smiling. "Call me or come over, whatever you want."

In Tully's station wagon for the trip home were Cap, Candy, Bobby Jo, Ben, Hoot, and Gabe. Everyone was in a mood to celebrate except Tully, who drove without contributing to the happy chatter.

"You guys looked real tough out there today," Gabe said. "I think you outplayed the Cobras, and they have a deeper bench, with a twelve-man roster."

"Nine good players can beat twelve not-so-good players," Candy pointed out, echoing her brother's pregame thoughts.

"Some of those Cobras are plenty good," Ben observed. "I'd take Vernon Dewey for my team any day."

"And their quarterback can throw," Cap pointed out. "But we did all right, huh, Grandpa?"

"You did fine," Tully replied. "All of you did real well."

"Cap, you can throw too," said Bobby Jo. "You were the best quarterback I saw today."

"Right!" echoed Candy. "When you don't get bomb-crazy, anyway."

Cap glared at his sister. "What's *that* supposed to mean?"

"Oh, come on, bro, you love those long, long passes! And they tend to be too long for human beings to get to, sometimes."

"Hey, I got us both touchdowns today! And neither of them was on a long pass!" Cap was angry.

Candy held up a hand. "Chill out, Cap."

"Don't tell me to chill out! And when I want you to tell me what I do wrong, I'll ask. If I don't ask, keep your opinions to yourself!"

Candy was startled at her brother's anger. "All I meant was —"

"I don't *care* what you meant," Cap broke in. "And I don't care what you think, either!"

Candy settled back in her seat, and no one spoke for several miles. Ben broke the silence.

"Well, I think Candy was right about *one* thing. Cap was the best quarterback out there today. Jimmy doesn't have the arm."

"And he doesn't play much defense," Hoot added. "Whatever that Mr. Cash says."

Tully slapped the steering wheel. "Cut it out, right now, all of you! I don't like hearing teammates knocking other teammates, and I don't want to hear it again, is that clear?"

"Yes sir," said Hoot, looking down at his shoes.

"Sorry," Ben muttered, his face flushed.

"That goes for you, too, Candy, Bobby Jo," Tully continued. "You ought to have better sense, especially with your coach sitting right here listening to it all."

"Sorry, Grandpa," said Candy.

"As for you, Cap, you should know better than to talk to your sister like that. The fact is that she has as good a head for football as *you* do. Maybe better."

Cap nodded and muttered an apology.

"Now, for the rest of this trip, I don't want to hear

any more arguing," Tully said, "and I *never* want to hear any member of this team sniping at a teammate. In fact, I don't even want you to *think* bad thoughts about your teammates. It's a sure way for a team to fall apart."

There wasn't much talk at all for the rest of the trip back to Cowpen.

Dinner at the Wadell house was quiet too, with Candy and Cap refusing to speak to each other and Tully not wanting conversation either. Sable had called and was due to come by after the meal.

"Excuse me," said Tully, getting up with his coffee cup and walking away from the table.

"Huh," said Cap, watching his grandfather leave the room. "Guess he's not looking forward to Mr. Cash coming over, is he."

Candy looked straight ahead and didn't reply.

"Oh, I guess you're not talking to me, is that it?" said Cap.

She turned to give Cap a cool look. "I thought you weren't interested in my opinions."

Cap turned red. "I didn't mean . . . that is, I wasn't . . . I *asked* for your opinion just now, didn't I?"

"Oh, I see," Candy said, still frosty. "It's only about *football* that you don't want to hear my opinions. But now you're willing to hear what I have to say?"

Cap fumbled for an answer. "It's not that I don't want —"

"I've been your biggest fan all along," Candy interrupted. "I keep telling you that you should be the starter and not Jimmy. You didn't mind hearing *those* opinions. Only when I have something to say that isn't a compliment, you want me to keep my mouth shut."

"Yeah. I mean . . . well, no . . . oh, I don't know what I'm saying. I shouldn't have gone off that way before. I was out of line. Guess I'm nervous about whether I'll get to start or not and I got touchy."

"I'll say you did," Candy said, but her look got milder. "I'm always on your side, and you ought to know that."

"Yeah, I know you are." Cap spread out his hands. "I won't let it happen any more, all right?"

"You better not," Candy said, scowling. Then she broke into a sunny smile. "Okay, apology accepted."

They heard the sound of an engine as someone drove up in front of their house.

"Must be Mr. Cash," Candy said.

"I wonder what he wants to say to Grandpa," said Cap. The window that opened on to the front porch was ajar.

"We shouldn't eavesdrop," Candy warned. "That isn't nice."

"Oh, no, that wouldn't be right," Cap agreed. "But if we sort of stayed real quiet, and *accidentally* heard something . . ."

"Accidentally, right," said Candy. "Can't blame us for an accident." The two sat where they were, not making a sound.

They heard a door slam and then their grandpa's voice. "Sable, come on up and sit."

A moment later, Tully spoke again. "What's on your mind?"

"You know what's on my mind," Sable Cash answered. "Who are you going to start at quarterback?"

"Not that it's really your business, but right now I'm leaning toward starting Cap."

Silently, Candy turned and gave her brother a thumbs-up sign.

They could clearly hear Sable's snort of anger.

"Now why am I not surprised that you picked your *grandson* over Jimmy."

Tully's voice got very quiet, which Cap knew was a sure sign that he was really angry.

"You saying I chose him because he's family? You think that's the kind of man I am?"

Sable came right back, also sounding hot. "Are *you* saying you think your grandson is a better quarterback than Jimmy?"

"Jimmy is a good athlete, but Cap's better on defense and —"

"Jimmy can move the ball! He'd never throw those long passes over everybody's head! And he'll get better on defense!"

A scrape of wood on wood told Cap that Tully had gotten up out of his chair.

"And Cap will learn to control his passing. He can throw short too!"

"Not with *you* coaching this team, he won't!" Now Sable had stood up. Cap and Candy exchanged a worried look. Was this going to get out of hand?

"If you don't like the way I'm coaching this team," Tully snapped, "you don't have to hang around anymore! It's bad enough the way you make the boys uncomfortable, sniping at me and taking shots at Cap. If you want to help me out anymore, you better put a lid on that!"

"Wadell, you haven't changed one bit since we were kids!" Sable was almost yelling now. "You thought you were hot stuff then and you still do! And I was a better quarterback than you any day of the week!"

Tully laughed. "That still sticks in your throat, doesn't it? That we won the championship and you didn't. Like I said, Cash, if you want to work with this team —"

"Oh, you bet I do! *Somebody's* got to teach 'em some sense, and it won't be you!"

"Then remember what I say!" Tully cut the other man off with a roar. "Concentrate on being a coach, and don't hassle the kids or me! Cap is going to start the first game and the subject is *closed!*"

Sable's voice was headed away from the house and back to his truck. "You're as stubborn as you are wrong-headed, Wadell! All right, *let* your grandson start. But I won't be responsible for what happens!"

"That's right, Cash, you won't!"

Cap and Candy heard the door of Sable's pickup slam and the engine roar to life.

A moment later, as Sable drove off with a squeal of tires, Tully stomped into the dining room to find Cap and Candy staring at him.

"Been listening in, have you?" he demanded.

"Us?" Candy asked, her eyes wide. "We were just sitting here talking."

"We *did* hear something, Grandpa," Cap added, "but it was kind of hard *not* to."

Tully was angry, but Cap saw that he wasn't angry at them.

"I guess you heard me say that I'm going to start you in the game against Sandville."

Cap nodded.

"And I hope you know that it's not because you're my grandson. It's because I think you're a little bit better than Jimmy, all things considered."

"He sure is," Candy agreed.

"I'll do the best I can," said Cap. "And . . . thanks."

"You give it everything you have and that'll be all the thanks I need." Tully paused for a moment. "You

78

know, Sable played for Sandville. Maybe that's why he really wanted Jimmy to start that game, I don't know. But if he gives you any trouble, just remember that it's not *you* he's mad at. It's *me*."

"I wish he'd get over it," Cap said.

"Well, you just concentrate on doing your job. I'll handle Sable. If we win this game, that'll shut him up."

Cap put a smile on his face, but to himself he thought, What if we lose?

On the Friday afternoon of the game, the Sandville 'Cudas showed up in a yellow school bus leading a fleet of cars and trucks full of fans. The bleachers were almost half full of Cowpen fans, including Candy, Bobby Jo, and Gabe Muñoz, along with friends and family of the other Panthers.

The 'Cudas got off their bus, already in their black-and-maroon uniforms. From where the Panthers were warming up, Cap took a look at his opponents. Sandville had *thirteen* players. His mouth felt dry. The 'Cudas ran out to the other end of the field and began doing calisthenics: jumping jacks, sit-ups, and so on. They looked . . . *ready.*

"They don't look so great," said Jimmy Cash, coming up behind Cap. "We can beat these guys."

A few days before, when Tully had told the team

that Cap would start, Jimmy had made a point of coming over and shaking his hand.

"Good luck. And I just want you to know, I don't believe your grandpa played favorites — whatever Gramps says."

Cap had been grateful to Jimmy. During the practices before the game, Tully and Sable had not spoken to each other except when it was necessary. Sable continued to help players and make suggestions, and Tully let him, knowing that Sable's advice was useful.

The referee for the game was a high school gym teacher from Ausburg, in a real ref's outfit with black-and-white-striped shirt and bright yellow flag to throw for penalties. A real ref, a real crowd . . . a *real game.* It was what Cap had wanted to play for years, almost since he could walk.

He felt weird, and couldn't tell whether he was excited, or nervous, or just plain scared. All those people in the bleachers . . . when he'd put on the blue-and-gold uniform, it felt funny. He had walked past a mirror and was startled at what he looked like.

He looked like a football player.

Sandville won the coin toss and chose to receive.

Hoot kicked off for the Panthers. His kick was short, but it took a bounce that the 'Cudas had trouble picking up. They wound up starting from their twenty-yard line. On their first series, they hit a short pass for six yards, but Ben and Mick stopped a run up the middle for a loss. Ben rushed the passer on third and eight and forced him to release the ball too quickly. The pass was incomplete and Sandville had to punt. The Cowpen fans cheered.

Hoot fielded the punt at the Cowpen nineteen, got a good block from Fritz, and ran it back to the thirty. The Panthers huddled and Cap called for a pass over the middle to Mick.

The blockers gave Cap time to set up, but his pass was a bullet and bounced off Mick's fingers, incomplete. On second down, Cap faked a long pass to Sam and shoveled an underhand throw to Ben, who plunged into the line, caught the 'Cudas by surprise, and gained nine yards. Cowpen third and six.

Cap called for another pass, sending Sam deep and Mick over the middle. He dropped back, saw that Sam had beaten his defender by two whole steps, and fired a long pass — *too* long. It sailed over Sam's head.

Cap had to punt. He noticed Sable Cash saying something to Tully, who shook his head and looked annoyed.

Cap's punt was high and forced the 'Cuda receiver back to his seven-yard line. Mick and Hoot dropped him just as he caught the ball.

This time the 'Cudas managed to gain some yards, but their drive was stopped at midfield when Cap picked off a pass. Cowpen had the ball on their thirty-five.

Tully sent in Vince to give Hoot a rest. Cap tossed a pitchout to Vince then blocked a 'Cuda defender. Behind Fritz's block, Vince got loose for ten yards. But another running play was stopped for no gain, and Cap's third-down pass, intended for Sam, was overthrown again.

The game was scoreless until the middle of the second quarter, when the 'Cudas tried a trick play. They completed a short pass to an end, and as the Panthers converged to bring him down, the end flipped the ball back to a trailing runner, who outran everyone into the end zone.

A placekick after the touchdown was perfect, and Sandville led, 8–0.

With three minutes left in the first half, Tully sent Jimmy in for Cap.

"About time," growled Sable. Cap figured Sable hadn't meant for him to hear, but he had. But he remembered what Tully had said and tried to concentrate on the game, shouting encouragement to Jimmy and his teammates.

Jimmy started off with an end-around, pitching to Sam as he circled around from his right-end position before racing downfield behind blocks from Ben, Steve, and Jimmy himself. Before the 'Cudas could run Sam down, he had gained twenty-four yards, and the ball was on the Sandville twenty-one. Two short passes brought them to the seven-yard line, and the Cowpen fans were all standing and yelling. On first and goal, Jimmy flipped the ball back to Fritz, but Fritz didn't run; he stepped back and threw into the end zone, where Sam pulled it in for six points.

Hoot kicked it through the uprights and the game was tied at eight apiece when the first half ended.

The teams headed for the gym locker rooms for the fifteen-minute halftime break. Most of the Panthers were excited and chattering to one another, although Cap had to force himself to join in. He slapped Jimmy on the back.

"Good job! You got us back in the game!" Jimmy smiled happily.

Hoot came over to Cap and spoke quietly. "You were a little nervous, that's all. You'll get 'em in the second half."

Cap hoped that he would have the chance to show what he could do in the second half but wondered if he would.

"All right, attention over here," Tully called out, and the Panthers settled down. "You did all right out there, and we can beat these guys if we play our game and keep our heads."

He tapped his clipboard. "Jimmy, good job mixing up the plays just then. You unsettled their defense. You'll start the second half. The other starters will be Ben, Hoot, Mick, Fritz, and Sam."

Cap hoped his disappointment didn't show, but he had to admit that he deserved to stay on the bench. He had done a pretty bad job.

Tully and Sable each gave short pep talks, telling

the Panthers to stay alert on defense and to remember the trick play that had got the 'Cudas their touchdown.

"It's important to see everything," Sable pointed out. "You see a running back trailing a receiver after a pass, think about what he's doing there. Don't commit to a tackle too soon!"

"Okay, we receive to start the second half," Tully said. "Let's get some more points on the board. Jimmy, the shovel pass to Ben might work again, so look for a place to use it. The main thing is to give it your best shot. Okay, Panthers. Ready to play ball?"

"*Yeah!*" they shouted and ran out of the locker room, fired up.

Hoot took the opening kickoff, and with the help of a few good blocks and one fine cutback, got all the way to the Panther thirty-eight before the 'Cudas stopped him. Jimmy gained six yards on a short pass to Mick and five more on a lateral to Fritz, who cut upfield and plowed over two tacklers. With third and four from the 'Cuda thirty-one, he tried a pass to Sam going deep, but his throw was high and short and a 'Cuda defender intercepted it.

Sandville struck quickly, gaining fifteen yards on a pass when Jimmy couldn't stay with his receiver. It was clear to Cap, watching from the sidelines, that the 'Cuda quarterback figured that Jimmy was a weak defensive link. He threw another pass good for twelve yards, once again taking advantage of Jimmy's not being able to cover his man tightly enough.

Sandville was now at midfield. Tully sent Vince in to replace Mick and to give Jimmy a message: Don't react too quickly when a receiver seems to be making a move; watch out for fakes.

Sandville tried the flea-flicker, the trick play that had gotten them their touchdown, but this time Hoot saw the running back trailing the receiver and hit him as soon as he caught the lateral, stopping the play for a gain of only five.

Jimmy got burned on another pass play, good for twenty yards, and Sandville was at the Cowpen fifteen.

On the sidelines, Cap tried to catch Tully's eye. He *knew* he'd do a better job than Jimmy on defense. But Tully didn't send him in. On the next play, the Sandville quarterback pitched it to another back — who threw it into the end zone where a receiver was waiting, all alone.

Jimmy had charged in too quickly, expecting a running play.

On the extra-point try, the snap was off target. The holder, a running back, picked it up and, dodging two tacklers, took it in. Sandville led, 15–8.

12

Cap wanted desperately to get back into the game, but Tully stayed with Jimmy. Jimmy showed that he could move the team and didn't attempt any more long passes. Mixing up short passes over the middle and sideline patterns, with a few runs, he marched the Panthers down the field to the 'Cuda ten-yard line. But a pass on third and four was knocked down, incomplete. Tully signaled for a time-out, and Cap listened as Jimmy talked to Tully and Sable.

"I'll get a first down," Jimmy insisted.

"Let him give it a shot," advised Sable.

But Tully shook his head. "We're within Hoot's field-goal range. Let's get four points."

Despite Sable's objections, Tully ordered the field-goal attempt. Hoot's kick was straight and long enough, and the Panthers trailed by only 15–12.

As Cowpen prepared to kick off, Cap tapped Tully's shoulder. "Uh . . . am I going to get another chance?"

Tully turned and said, "You'll get back in, don't worry."

Hoot kicked it deep, but the 'Cuda blockers opened a hole in the middle, and the return man almost broke the runback for a touchdown. Hoot, the kicker, was the last man with a chance to bring him down. He barely did it, making a shoetop tackle, at the Panther twenty.

Tully sent Cap in to play defense, bringing Jimmy to the sidelines. On first down, the 'Cudas tried a short-pass play to a runner coming out of the backfield. Cap reacted quickly and lunged in front of the receiver, getting a hand on the ball and deflecting it. Second down. The Sandville quarterback pitched out to a runner, who threw a short pass to the center. Hoot read the play and slammed into the center just as the ball reached him, stopping him for a gain of just one yard and making it third and fourteen.

In the Panther defensive huddle, Cap said, "They're going to have to throw for the first down. Let's try to pressure the quarterback."

The Panthers lined up two rushers, one on either side of the center, and they charged into the backfield just as the ball was snapped. The 'Cuda passer, seeing Ben and Fritz thundering down on him, threw a hasty pass that wasn't close to anybody. They called time with a fourth down and long yardage to get.

In came their placekicker. "Think he can kick it that far?" Sam asked Cap.

"Maybe it's a fake," Cap replied. "Watch out."

It wasn't a fake, and the kick was good. Sandville had built its lead back up to 19–12.

Cap was disappointed when Tully sent Jimmy back out to run the offense. A voice from the bleachers yelled out, "Keep Cap in there!" It sounded to Cap like his sister, but he wasn't sure.

Sable walked over to Tully and said, "You did the right thing, bringing Jimmy in. He'll get us the lead back, you watch."

Tully didn't answer.

The 'Cuda kickoff was deep into the end zone for a touchback, and Cowpen took over at their twenty. Jimmy surprised the Sandville defense with a reverse, on which he pitched to Fritz running toward right end. Fritz handed off to Sam coming around to the left. The 'Cudas, caught by surprise, didn't recover and catch Sam until he had gained twenty-five yards, getting into Sandville territory.

The Cowpen fans yelled encouragement. Sable flashed a grin at Tully. "What'd I tell you?"

Jimmy then fired a quick pass to Mick, who picked up ten yards before being brought down at the twenty-five. After an incomplete pass, it was third and five. Jimmy dropped back to throw, but this time the 'Cudas had his receivers covered. There were no defenders on the line, and Jimmy cradled the ball and began to run.

The ref tossed his yellow flag and blew his whistle, stopping play.

"Running play without a clear pass, that'll cost you five yards and the down."

Jimmy's embarrassment could be seen from the sidelines. Cap felt bad for him. Tully beckoned Cap over.

"We're out of field-goal range, so go in and punt. Angle it for the sidelines. Let's try to pin 'em back against their goal line."

Cap ran in, and Jimmy, seeing him, started out. As

they met, Cap said, "It could've been me who forgot that rule, just as easy as you. We're still new at this game."

Jimmy smiled at Cap. "Thanks."

Cap took Ben's snap and aimed his kick at the sidelines. The ball sailed out of bounds, and the ref ruled that it had gone out at the Sandville ten. Cap looked over to Tully, who nodded and gave him a thumbs-up sign. He also kept Cap in the game. Before Sandville could run a play, the ref signaled the end of the third quarter.

The teams went to the sidelines to catch their breath and plan for the fourth period.

Sable nudged Tully. "You'll put Jimmy back in for offense, right?"

Tully looked around at the players, all of whom had heard what Sable said, and snapped. "This isn't the time for that. Let's concentrate on getting the ball back in good field position."

"But —" started Sable.

Tully cut him off fast. *"No buts!* I'll talk to you later."

He turned to the players. "Listen up. They're deep in their territory and I'm guessing they won't want to risk an interception. I figure they'll try to make some short gains with running plays. So watch out for them. Sam, stay back deep and watch for receivers, in case I'm wrong. The rest of you, think *run*. Let's try to hold 'em where they are so they'll give us good field position when they punt. Ben, Mick, Fritz, stay close to the line. Cap, Hoot, you're our roving linebackers."

As the Panthers took the field, Cap saw Tully wheel around and say something angry to Sable, who snapped right back. Great, he thought. Just what we need. Jimmy, he noted, had moved as far away from the quarreling grandfathers as he could get.

Sure enough, on first down, Sandville tried a pitchout and a sweep around right end. The 'Cuda blockers took out Mick and Fritz, but Ben and Hoot got through the interference and nailed the runner at the line of scrimmage, setting up a second and fifteen.

On second down, the Sandville quarterback dropped back as if to pass. The fastest 'Cuda took off on a deep-pass pattern, with Sam staying with him. But instead of passing, the quarterback flipped the ball to a running back behind him. The back plunged straight ahead and was tackled by Ben and Cap for a one-yard loss.

On third and sixteen, Tully sent in Steve for Mick, and Steve told the other Panthers to watch for a possible pass play.

But this time, the 'Cudas caught Cowpen by surprise. The quarterback retreated a few steps and punted. With no one back deep to receive the quick kick, the ball bounced and rolled all the way to the Cowpen eighteen, where Sam fell on the ball. Cap admitted that the quick kick had been a smart play. After all, Sandville had the lead, and the clock was running.

Jimmy ran onto the field, and Cap, wishing he could have another shot on offense, ran off. But Jimmy managed to get only one first down, and the Panthers were forced to punt again.

Cap came back in on defense, wondering if he was doomed to play only defense for the rest of the season. The 'Cudas were on their twenty and picked up fifteen yards on a deep sideline pass. Cap looked at the clock at the end of the field. If Sandville scored again, he realized, it'd be hard for Cowpen to get the lead back in the little time remaining.

The next play, however, was a pass over the middle that Hoot intercepted and ran back to the Panther thirty. Jimmy came back in and threw a short pass to Vince for four yards. Cap felt a tap on the shoulder, and Tully spoke into his ear.

"Cap, go in for Jimmy. We need to score, and time's running out. Go in and air it out, son."

Heart pounding, Cap raced out and took over for Jimmy. He called for Sam to go deep. "Guys, you gotta give me time to get this one off," he urged.

"Don't worry," Ben said, and Fritz nodded his agreement.

Taking the snap, Cap dropped back five quick steps. He saw Ben slam into one 'Cuda, while Fritz cut another defender down with a beautiful block. Meanwhile, Sam was sprinting downfield, a Sandville player trying desperately to keep up.

Don't overthrow this one, he told himself as he cocked his arm and let the ball fly.

Sam caught it over his shoulder and raced into the end zone. The Panthers were within a single point!

Tully signaled for a time-out and waved Cap and Hoot over. "If we run or pass it in, we tie the game. If Hoot kicks it, we're ahead by a point, with less than two minutes left."

"Let's go for the win," said Hoot.

"Right," Cap said. He noticed that Sable wasn't taking part in the conversation. He was standing by himself, scowling.

Tully grinned. "All right, let's go for it."

Cap and Hoot ran back out. "This should be easy," Cap said.

"I'll give it my best shot," replied Hoot.

The Panthers lined up and Ben snapped the ball to Cap, who was the holder. Cap fumbled the ball slightly, but managed to get it down just as Hoot swung his foot into the ball.

The ball sailed to the right of the goalposts. Cowpen still trailed by one point, with very little time left.

Hoot dropped to his knees, the picture of misery. Cap knelt next to him.

"C'mon, Hoot, it's all right. Hey, if you hadn't intercepted that pass, we wouldn't have even gotten back into this game. Look, I've messed up a lot more than you today. And it's not over yet. There's still time left."

But there wasn't enough time. The 'Cudas knew that Cowpen had only one time-out remaining and managed to get a first down and run out the clock. The final score was Sandville 19, Cowpen 18.

The unhappy Panthers trudged off the field just in time to see Sable run up to Tully.

"If you'd put Jimmy in sooner and kept him in we could have won this game!"

Tully just kept walking, not saying a word.

But Sable wouldn't let up. "A fine coach you are! We should've won that game!"

Finally, Tully spun around and glared at Sable. "That's enough! I'm sick and tired of you getting on me all the time, and in front of the kids, too! You're embarrassing Jimmy, as well as everybody else. *I'm* still coaching this team, and if you don't like it, then stay away!"

Sable was about to yell back, but Jimmy grabbed his arm. *"Gramps!* Please stop!"

Sable looked at Jimmy in surprise. The boy's face was red, and he looked as if he might start to cry any second.

"Jimmy . . . I . . . I was standing up for you, boy. I was speaking out for you!"

"Well, I don't *want* you to!" Jimmy stared hard at Sable. "So stop, Gramps. *Please!*"

Sable opened his mouth and closed it again. He looked around at the other Panthers, but none of them would meet his eyes.

"I'll see you when you're ready to go home, Jimmy," he said, and walked away.

Tully sighed and clapped his hands to get the team's attention. "All right, boys, I'm sorry about that, but it's just something between Mr. Cash and me, and nothing to do with you. I think you played a good game today, and we could as easily have won as lost.

"Next week, we play Moosetown, and we should focus on that and on getting a win under our belts. I'll see you all at practice on Monday. Someone has to lose every game but don't let it get you down. Okay?"

Tully looked around. "Now, who's coming with me? I have to get home and do a few errands."

As Cap turned to leave, Jimmy ran over to him.

"You don't think that I believe what Gramps said, do you? Because I *don't.* I think he was wrong to say it."

Cap smiled at Jimmy. "I know you don't think that way. Grandpa is right — this is something between the two of them. It has nothing to do with you and me. Really."

Jimmy smiled back, relieved, and waved at Cap as he went after his grandfather. "See you Monday!"

During the week before the Moosetown game, Sable didn't show up until Wednesday. When he did, he asked Tully if he could speak to him, and the two men talked quietly in private. Afterward, Sable resumed his coaching but was very careful not to start any arguments or say anything that was critical of Tully as a coach or of any players.

Tully decided not to introduce many new plays but to keep drilling the Panthers in what they already knew. But he did add one wrinkle: putting Cap and Jimmy in at the same time, so that one of them could either run or throw a halfback option pass.

He also tried to help Jimmy with his pass defense, explaining how he might avoid getting tricked by a receiver's feints and not get drawn out of position.

On Friday, at the end of practice, he gathered the team around him.

"Tomorrow we leave for Moosetown at three o'clock. Everybody get plenty of rest, and let's be ready to play a great game tomorrow."

Early on the morning of the game it rained hard for several hours, but the rain ended by noon, and the sun was shining brightly when Cap and Tully came outside.

"Looks like a great day to play," Tully said, shading his eyes and looking around.

Mrs. Wadell, Cap's mother, came out on the front porch. "Water is flooding all over the back garden. I think the rain gutters got full of dead leaves last night. Since Dad's already left for the fields, could you and Cap clean the gutters out?"

"Sure thing," Tully replied. "Cap, let's haul out the ladder and get to it." They dragged the metal extension ladder out of the basement and leaned it against the edge of the roof over the front porch. As Cap held the ladder to steady it, Tully climbed up with a water hose and washed the collected leaves out of the gutter.

They carried the ladder around to the back of the house, and Tully once again hauled the hose up to the roofline. But as he hosed out the gutter, Tully saw that the branch of a nearby tree kept him from being able to reach the end of the trough with the stream of water from the hose. Rather than climb back down and move the ladder, he tried to stretch out and lean himself around the branch.

Suddenly the top of the ladder slid to the side and Tully fell off into the branches of the tree, and from there to the ground, where he landed with a thump.

"Grandpa!" Cap yelled, running over to Tully and kneeling down. "Are you okay?"

"I think so, just help me up," Tully muttered. Mrs. Wadell ran out into the yard.

"What was that noise? What happened? Tully, are you all right?"

Tully struggled to his feet and winced. "My shoulder . . . I must have done something to my shoulder . . . can't move my arm too good."

"Do you think it's broken?" asked Cap.

"Come on," Mrs. Wadell said. "I'm driving you to the hospital emergency room."

"But . . . the game . . ." stammered Tully.

"Never mind that," Mrs. Wadell snapped. "Let's see to that arm."

"All right, just give me one minute. Cap, call Hoot and Ben and tell them they'll have to get over to the game without me. And you can hitch a ride with them."

Cap shook his head. "I'll call them, but I'm coming with you."

"Hurry and make those calls," Mrs. Wadell told her son. "We should have the arm looked at quickly. And leave a message telling Candy where we went."

A few minutes later, the Wadells were in the station wagon, headed for the local hospital.

"The game doesn't start until four," Tully said. "We'll get there in plenty of time — even if my arm is in a cast."

But the emergency room was jammed, and the doctor didn't see Tully for over an hour. He examined Tully's arm and shoulder and sent him off for X-rays.

A while later, the doctor came back, smiling. "Tully, you're a lucky man, even if you pulled a dumb stunt with that ladder. Nothing's broken. You have some bad bruises and strained muscles, but you'll be as good as new in a week or so. Try to be more careful on ladders from now on, unless you want to spend more time in this place."

"Thanks, Doc," Tully said, looking at his watch and frowning. "It's three o'clock already, and Moosetown is an hour away. Maybe if we hurry we can get there by halftime."

Cap struck his hand to his head. "I didn't bring my uniform!" he cried. "Now we have to go get it and then drive to Moosetown."

"We'll get there for part of the game, anyway," Tully said, as they hurried out to the station wagon. They headed back home, where Candy and Bobby Jo were waiting anxiously.

Candy said, "Grandpa, how are you? We've been so worried!"

"It's nothing much, just some bruises," Tully said, looking out the car window. "Cap, get your uniform, quick, and let's get moving. Candy, Bobby Jo, hop in the back. We're late!"

Cap struggled into his pads and jersey as they drove to Moosetown and quickly finished dressing when they arrived. Going as fast as Tully's injured arm would let them, they headed for the football field. There were about a hundred people in the bleachers, but the field itself was empty.

"Must be halftime," Tully said.

Cap looked around for the rest of the Panthers. "I wonder how we're doing." Then he saw the wooden scoreboard on the side of the field. It read MOOSE-TOWN STEERS 20. COWPEN PANTHERS 0.

"Oh, no," he groaned. "We're way behind."

Candy pointed to one end of the field. "There they are, Grandpa, look!"

The Panthers sat in a circle around Sable Cash, who seemed to be giving a pep talk. He stopped when he saw Tully, Cap, and the others headed in their direction.

"Tully!" Sable shouted. "How are you doing? Man, it's good to see you!" He pulled the whistle from around his neck and offered it to Tully. "You feeling good enough to take over? Because I'm ready to retire from coaching as of now!"

"What's the problem, Sable?" Tully asked. "Is the Moosetown team that good?"

"Yes . . . well, not really . . . I don't know!" Sable said. "All I know is, I'd rather you took over and tried to get us back into this game, if it's all right with you."

Tully looked over to where the Moosetown Steers, wearing green-and-white uniforms, were listening to their coach. "They don't look any better than us, as far as I can tell. Who's getting the ball to open the third quarter?"

"We are," said Jimmy.

"All right," Tully said. "Jimmy, you start at quarterback."

Cap hid his disappointment.

"Cap, you're going to start as a running back with Hoot," Tully continued. "Sam, Ben, and Mick will be in the line. We're going to show 'em our secret weapon — the halfback option. It'll mess up their minds."

Sure enough, when the Panthers started on offense from their twenty-two, Jimmy pitched to Cap, who fired a strike to Sam that was good for fifteen yards and a first down. On the next play, Jimmy pitched again and two receivers went deep. But this time Cap took off with the ball and Ben and Mick provided key blocks. He gained twelve more yards, putting the ball on the Steer thirty-one.

On the next play, Cap hit Sam, who had gotten behind the Moosetown secondary, and Sam took it in for a touchdown. Hoot kicked straight and true and the Panthers were on the scoreboard, trailing 20–8.

The Steers came out on offense looking less confident. With the ball on their twenty-five, they tried a pitchout to a running back. But Ben broke through the line and picked it off, rumbling down to the eight before being dragged down from behind. Jimmy threw Ben a shovel pass on the Panthers' first play and caught the Steers by surprise. Ben forced his way into the end zone, and Hoot kicked the conversion.

With two minutes left in the third quarter, the score was Steers 20, Panthers 16.

But the Steers came back on their next possession, driving down the field with a well-controlled short-yardage offense that ate up a lot of time and resulted in a touchdown. Their placekicker had hurt his ankle, so they ran in the extra point to extend their lead to 27–16. There were four and a half minutes left in the fourth quarter.

Mick fielded the Moosetown kickoff on his ten,

and dodged and twisted his way to the thirty. Now Tully brought Cap in as quarterback and Jimmy in as a running back. Cap pitched to Jimmy, and he, Fritz, and Ben opened a gaping hole. Jimmy darted into the secondary, faked a Moosetown player beautifully, and picked up fifteen yards and a first down.

Jimmy came out and Hoot returned. Cap faked a pitchout to him, spun, and fired a bullet pass that Mick caught for a gain of five more. The ball was on the Moosetown thirty, and there were three minutes left. Cowpen needed two scores to win. Jimmy raced back in, sending Hoot to the bench.

"Coach says we need to score fast," said Jimmy as he reached the huddle.

Cap grinned as an idea came to him. "Remember the flea-flicker Sandville used last week? Let's try it on these guys." He whispered a few instructions and the Panthers came to the line. On the snap, Cap dropped back and fired a short pass to Sam, who turned and lateraled back to Jimmy, trailing him by a few yards.

Jimmy put on a burst of speed and suddenly it was a footrace to the end zone, with Jimmy being chased by two Steers. But Jimmy got there first. The

Panthers were back in the game! When Hoot kicked the conversion, Moosetown led by only three.

But there were just two and a half minutes left to play.

The Steers tried to use up the remaining time with short passes and running plays. They got as far as midfield, where Ben's crunching tackle knocked the ball out of a Moosetown runner's hands. Mick fell on the ball, and the Panthers had one more chance . . . and thirty-five seconds on the clock.

Tully called a time-out and waved Cap over to talk to him. "We can win with a field goal," he said. "You don't have to go for the end zone; just get within range for Hoot to kick. Inside the twenty would be good enough, though closer would be better. We only have one time-out left, so don't run the ball, pass it. Incomplete passes stop the clock."

Cap called a pass play that sent three receivers out but saw as he dropped back that Moosetown was in a prevent defense designed to keep a play from going long. He threw to the only open man, Jimmy, who ran out of bounds, stopping the clock after gaining five yards.

On second and ten, with thirty seconds left, it

looked as if Sam had a step on his man. But Sam couldn't hang on to Cap's pass. With twenty-five seconds left, it was third down and ten yards needed for a first down.

The Steers rushed three men at Cap, forcing him to roll out to his right. He threw on the run, hitting Sam for a gain of ten. But Sam was tackled inbounds, meaning the clock was still running. Tully signaled for Cap to call the last Panther time-out. Cap went to the sidelines.

"We have eight seconds. Time enough to throw one long pass. If it's incomplete, Hoot'll have to kick."

Cap called a deep-pass play, but saw that Sam was surrounded by Moosetown defenders and threw the ball away.

He turned to Hoot. "It's up to you. Give it everything you've got."

Hoot looked nervous. "I never kicked one this long before."

The Panthers set up for the field goal try. Ben snapped the ball to Cap, who set it down perfectly. Hoot put all his strength into his kick and the ball sailed straight toward the goalposts. Cap watched it.

Come on, he thought, get there!

The ball hit the crossbar, bounced back, and rolled on the ground. The game was over and the Panthers had lost, 27–24.

As the cheering Steers and their fans celebrated, the dejected Cowpen players slowly walked off the field. Tully waited for them.

"You boys should be proud of yourselves," he said. "You were down by twenty at the half and you didn't give up on yourselves. You almost came all the way back. Good job!"

"They would have won this game if they'd had the right coach." Sable joined the group, looking unhappy.

"Gramps . . ." Jimmy began, but Sable held up his hand.

"No, Jimmy, the fact is, if Tully had coached the whole game, we'd never have been so far behind. He's a better coach than me and I want you all to know. I've been acting dumb for a couple of weeks, but I've learned my lesson." He cleared his throat and continued. "Tully's right. You boys played well, once he showed up. In fact, I think we should celebrate our comeback. Let's meet at the Spot for a postgame feed. Candy, Bobby Jo, Gabe, that includes you. It's my treat!"

There was a cheer from all the Panthers, and Cap and Jimmy grinned and exchanged high fives.

"However," Sable called out, "I *still* think we would've beat you if I hadn't broken my leg."

Tully stared at Sable and then laughed. "Maybe you would have, at that. But we'll never know. Now, let's head for Cowpen and feed these hungry Panthers!"

Matt Christopher

Sports Bio Bookshelf

Andre Agassi

John Elway

Wayne Gretzky

Ken Griffey Jr.

Mia Hamm

Grant Hill

Randy Johnson

Michael Jordan

Lisa Leslie

Tara Lipinski

Mark McGwire

Greg Maddux

Hakeem Olajuwon

Emmitt Smith

Sammy Sosa

Mo Vaughn

Tiger Woods

Steve Young

The #1 Sports Writer for Kids

Read them all!

- Baseball Flyhawk
- Baseball Pals
- Baseball Turnaround
- The Basket Counts
- Catch That Pass!
- Catcher with a Glass Arm
- Center Court Sting
- Challenge at Second Base
- The Comeback Challenge
- The Counterfeit Tackle
- Crackerjack Halfback
- The Diamond Champs
- Dirt Bike Racer
- Dirt Bike Runaway
- Double Play at Short

- Face-Off
- Fighting Tackle
- Football Fugitive
- The Fox Steals Home
- The Great Quarterback Switch
- The Hockey Machine
- Ice Magic
- Johnny Long Legs
- The Kid Who Only Hit Homers
- Long-Arm Quarterback
- Long Shot for Paul
- Long Stretch at First Base
- Look Who's Playing First Base
- Miracle at the Plate
- Mountain Bike Mania

No Arm in Left Field

Olympic Dream

Penalty Shot

Pressure Play

Prime-Time Pitcher

Red-Hot Hightops

The Reluctant Pitcher

Return of the Home Run Kid

Roller Hockey Radicals

Run, Billy, Run

Shoot for the Hoop

Shortstop from Tokyo

Skateboard Tough

Snowboard Maverick

Snowboard Showdown

Soccer Halfback

Soccer Scoop

Spike It!

The Submarine Pitch

Supercharged Infield

Tackle Without a Team

The Team That Couldn't Lose

Tight End

Too Hot to Handle

Top Wing

Touchdown for Tommy

Tough to Tackle

Wingman on Ice

The Winning Stroke

The Year Mom Won the Pennant

All available in paperback from Little, Brown and Company